Blueberry Bear

Blue Dogs
Rule!

Blueberry Bear

A Furry Friends Tale

written by Eileen Pieczonka

illustrated by Romi Caron

To all rescues and wannabe Flatties.
May you feel loved and find your forever homes.

~ ep

For everyone who knows what it is to love a dog,
and for those who will discover it.

~rc

The text is set in Papyrus

10 9 8 7 6 5 4 3 2 1
First Edition

Children/Animals/Dogs

ISBN-13: 978-0-692-14367-4

Illustrations by Romi Caron
Cover and book design by Naomi C. Rose

 Blueberry Bear Tales
Phoenix, Arizona
www.blueberrybeartales.com

Printed in United States

Somewhere, out there, is a friend for me.

Somehow, someway, I must break free.

I'm teased for being blueberry blue.

I wish for a buddy, dear and true.

No fence is TALL enough, or W I D E enough, to keep this pup in. Blueberry Bear ALWAYS finds a way out.

4

ZIP, ZOOM.

Swish, swash.

Sniff, sniff.

What's out there?

Blueberry Bear leaps and soars.

Fa-thump, bumpity, bump, bump!

Blueberry Bear slides
past sunflowers,
and rose bushes,
and a tree with a swing.

Closer, and closer, and.......

KURPOING!

"Yikes! A giant blueberry," shouts Hare.

"I'm no giant blueberry. I'm Blueberry Bear."

Sniff, sniff. "But you are not a bear," says Hare.

"My name is Bear, and I LOVE BLUEBERRIES.
Would you like to be my friend?" asks Blueberry Bear.

9

FWOOP! Hare's ears flatten back. "You are no friend of mine."
SLIP, SLIDE. Stones roll. Hare zippity hoppity bops away.

"Wait for Meeeeeeeeeee," yelps Blueberry Bear.

SNAP, CRACKLE, CRUNCH.

Blueberry Bear bolts

past moss,

and ferns,

and wild blueberries.

What's that gray and black, creeping from tree to tree? Trouble follows Blueberry Bear.

13

FA-LUMP, FA-LUMP, FA-LUMP. Blueberry Bear finally catches up.

SLIP, SLIDE. Leaves fly.

"Geez, you scared the jelly beans out of me," huffs Hare. "Now scoot."

"But why?" asks Blueberry Bear. "I just want to be friends."

"I see the wolf in you," says Hare. "Wolves are VERY dangerous. They hunt rabbits and hares."

"I'm no wolf," she yips. "I hunt blueberries, not bunny rabbits."

"Well, I am not any bunny. I am Tripper von Hare IV."

What's that gray and black, creeping from tree to tree?
Double trouble follows Blueberry Bear.

Whooooo, whoosh. The wind whirls and swirls.

Sniff, sniff. "Pee-yew! What stinks?" asks Blueberry Bear.

"Don't look at me," grumbles Tripper von Hare IV.

WHOOOOOOOOOOOOO

WHOOOOOSH

"Pssst. Little Missy." Sweet Pea waddles closer. "Just who are you call'n stinky? Didn't your mama teach you any manners?"

TH-THUMP, TH-THUMP, TH-THUMP. "This is going to be one bad hare day," mumbles Tripper von Hare IV.

"You got that right, Tripper," scolds Sweet Pea.

"I just want to be friends," whimpers Blueberry Bear.

What's that gray and black, creeping from tree to tree? Triple trouble follows Blueberry Bear. CRUNCH! "I'll be your friend," gruffs Wolf. Blueberry Bear's ears peak. "For real?" "Not Wolf!" gasp the animals.

Wolf slinks towards Blueberry Bear.

"Don't listen to them, Little One," snorts Wolf.

Blueberry Bear flips her head back. *Phew! Wolf's breath smells stinkier than Sweet Pea.*

"Wolf is tricking you," hollers Hare. "RUN Blueberry Bear. Run, before it's too late!"

Blueberry Bear scurries under Wolf.

Wolf turns and nips at her tail.

"Oh noooooooooooo, it's too late," cry the animals.

"Aroooooo," howls Wolf. He eyes Tripper von Hare IV.

"Oh nooooooooooooo, Wolf is on the hunt," scream the animals.

PITTER PATTER. Paws scatter.

Wolf leaps and charges.

Blueberry Bear jumps in Wolf's way. "Don't you dare hurt Hare."

"What are you going to do about it, Little One?" snarls Wolf.

Blueberry Bear flips like a Ninja.

Wolf steps back and away.

SPLASH!

Wolf races off, never looking back.

SPLASH

Skippity hop. Tripper von Hare IV dashes over.

"Wow! Where did you get those Kung Fu moves? You are one brave pup," says Hare.

"I wanted to keep you safe," says Blueberry Bear.

"Thanks, my friend," says Hare. "You can call me, Tripper."

Blueberry Bear's eyes widen. "FRIENDS!"

Tripper gives her a huge hare hug. "You are my truest, bluest,
Best-est Friend."
Blueberry Bear slops Tripper with kisses.
"Ewwwwww! Snout snoggers, dog germs, dog stink. YUCK!"
grunts Tripper.

They tumble to the ground and roll into wild blueberry bushes.
Blueberry Bear laughs, "Now you're just like me, blueberry blue."

ONOMATOPOEIA (ON-uh-MAT-uh-PEE-uh)

A word that phonetically imitates a designated noise or action. Used in literature, especially for children's books and poems. By incorporating onomatopoeia in her books, Eileen Pieczonka aims to engage her young audience with a delightful and entertaining read.

Air: swish, swash, whooo, whoosh

Animals: arooooo (dog or wolf)

Water: splash

Breaking: snap, crackle, crunch

Collision: Kurpoing

Flattening: Fwoop

Pounding: th-thump

Movement Sounds:

Running: fa-lump; pitter, patter

High Speed: zip, zoom

Falling: Fa-thump, bumpity, bump

Other: slip, slide, skippity hop

ACKNOWLEDGMENTS

A special thank you to Tracie Will for her Flat-coated Retriever aesthetic recommendations for Blueberry Bear.

Although Jamie was my inspiration for Blueberry Bear, it's the children that inspire me to keep writing. A pawsative thank you to my young readers who love Blueberry Bear.

Lastly, a big paws up to the winners of Blueberry Bear's Best in Show Writing Contest: Taylor, Crew, Isaiah, and Parker. These young writers have shown impressive writing skills, creativity, and passion. Last year, I awarded the winners with an autographed copy of Blueberry Bear at their Queen Creek Unified School District's Awards Ceremony.

To all students: Reading is fun. It also expands the imagination, and is the key to great writing.

IN MEMORY OF JAMIE (a.k.a. Blueberry Bear)

June 10, 2003 to January 17, 2018

Jamie enjoyed swimming and digging, library visits, book signings and special events, local car shows, trips to Sedona, and she was a foodie lover.

Jamie was a gentle loving soul who touched hundreds of lives, especially children's. Her deep amber eyes, beauty, and sweet disposition were magnetic. Jamie lived a true rags to riches life. From a young abused stray with four pups, to a reading therapy dog, to being my inspiration for Blueberry Bear. Jamie was one of many examples of how rescues fulfill lives in wondrous ways.

Sweet Dreams Blueberry Bear. You will always be remembered, loved, and missed.